S0-ABC-652

144330 EN
Tucker's Beetle Band

Feldman, Thea
ATOS BL 2.5
Points: 0.5   LG

Dear Parents and Teachers,

In an easy-reader format, **My Readers** introduce classic stories to children who are learning to read. Although favorite characters and time-tested tales are the basis for **My Readers**, the books tell completely new stories and are freshly and beautifully illustrated.

My Readers are available in three levels:

1 **Level One** is for the emergent reader and features repetitive language and word clues in the illustrations.

2 **Level Two** is for more advanced readers who still need support saying and understanding some words. Stories are longer with word clues in the illustrations.

3 **Level Three** is for independent, fluent readers who enjoy working out occasional unfamiliar words. The stories are longer and divided into chapters.

Encourage children to select books based on interests, not reading levels. Read aloud with children, showing them how to use the illustrations for clues. With adult guidance and rereading, children will eventually read the desired book on their own.

Here are some ways you might want to use this book with children:

- Talk about the title and the cover illustrations. Encourage the child to use these to predict what the story is about.
- Discuss the interior illustrations and try to piece together a story based on the pictures. Does the child want to change or adjust his first prediction?
- After children reread a story, suggest they retell or act out a favorite part.

My Readers will not only help children become readers, they will serve as an introduction to some of the finest classic children's books available today.

—LAURA ROBB
Educator and Reading Consultant

To my parents: Murray and Thelma
—T. F.

To Alla
—O. I. & A. I.

SQUARE
FISH

An Imprint of Macmillan Children's Publishing Group

HARRY CAT AND TUCKER MOUSE: TUCKER'S BEETLE BAND.
Text copyright © 2011 by Thea Feldman. Illustrations copyright © 2011 by Olga and Aleksey Ivanov.
All rights reserved. Distributed in Canada by H.B. Fenn and Company Ltd.
Printed in January 2011 in China by Toppan Leefung Printing Ltd., Dongguan City, Guangdong Province.
For information, address Square Fish, 175 Fifth Avenue, New York, NY 10010.

Library of Congress Cataloging-in-Publication Data Available

ISBN: 978-0-312-62575-7 (hardcover)
1 3 5 7 9 10 8 6 4 2

ISBN: 978-0-312-62576-4 (paperback)
1 3 5 7 9 10 8 6 4 2

Book design by Patrick Collins/Véronique Lefèvre Sweet

Square Fish logo designed by Filomena Tuosto

First Edition: 2011

www.squarefishbooks.com
www.mackids.com

This is a Level 2 book

LEXILE 500L

Harry Cat and Tucker Mouse
TUCKER'S BEETLE BAND

Story by Thea Feldman

Illustrated by Olga and Aleksey Ivanov

Inspired by the characters from
The Cricket in Times Square
written by George Selden and illustrated by Garth Williams

SQUARE
FISH

Macmillan Children's Publishing Group
New York

Tucker Mouse liked the everyday sounds
of the busy subway station
in Times Square.
He lived in a drainpipe there
with his best friend, Harry Cat.

Rumble went the trains.

Stomp, stomp went all the hurrying feet.

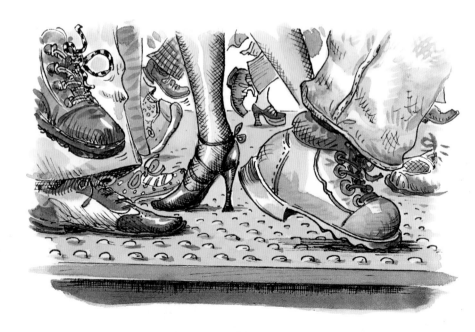

Cree, cree, cree went Chester Cricket.

He was Harry and Tucker's friend.

He lived at the newsstand

near the drainpipe.

At night, all the sounds stopped.

While Harry went out for adventures,

Tucker loved to fall asleep

in peace and quiet.

One day, four beetle musicians
started playing their music
directly below Harry and Tucker.
That night, when the other sounds
in the station stopped,
the beetle band did not.

Bang! Plink!

Shake, shake, shake!

La, la, la!

The music was so loud,

it shook poor Tucker's whiskers.

Tucker marched downstairs.

"Hello," sang one of the beetles.

"My name is Saul.

Do you like our music?"

"I'm Tucker Mouse," said Tucker.

"I live upstairs.

Your music is too loud.

You should not play at night!"

"We're sorry," said Saul,

"but we have to practice.

Next week, we're hoping to win

the Battle of the Bug Bands

at the flea market in Bryant Park.

You should come."

Saul handed Tucker a flyer.

"Battle of the Bug Bands,"
Tucker grumbled
as he went back upstairs.
"The winning band travels
around the country.
Big deal!"

Tucker stuffed two pieces
of the flyer in his ears.

But he could still feel the music
all the way from his ears
to his tail.

When Harry came home,

Tucker told him

all about the beetle band.

"Well," said Harry,

"if the beetle band won the contest,

they would go away.

Then it would be quiet again at night."

"But how can we make sure

the band wins?" asked Tucker.

Then he had an idea.

Tucker went back downstairs.

"I know a thing or two about talent," said Tucker.

"I will be your manager!"

"Great," said Saul.

"Let's shake on it!"

Shake, shake, shake!

19

Tucker worked with the band

for hours and hours.

One day, he invited Harry

and Chester Cricket to listen.

Harry and Chester
clapped and cheered.
"Bravo!" they shouted.

The next day, Tucker said,
"Tomorrow is the concert.
Let's take a break
and go for a run."
Tucker cheered as his beetles
jogged around the mailbox.

Suddenly, Saul tripped and fell!

"Ouch!" Saul cried.

"I think I have hurt my arms!

I don't think I can play tomorrow!"

The band tried their song without Saul.

Bang! Plink!

La, la, la!

Something was missing.

There wasn't time to find

another piece of music.

The beetle band was not going

to be able to play.

"This is all my fault!"

said Tucker.

"No, it's not," said Saul.

"You are the best manager ever."

That night, it was very quiet.

But Tucker didn't like that, after all.

Not if it meant his friends

had to give up their dream.

And the beetles had indeed

become Tucker's friends.

"Friends don't let each other down!"

he cried.

"I know someone who could help,"

said Harry.

Harry hurried to the newsstand.

"You're a cricket,

and crickets are bugs,"

he said to Chester.

"And you can play music.

Tucker and the beetle band

need your help!"

Chester was a shy bug,

but he agreed.

The next day, there was no time

for even a quick practice.

Everyone hurried to Bryant Park.

The Battle of the Bug Bands

was under way!

After other groups played,

the beetle band—

starring Chester Cricket—

took the stage.

Bang! Plink!

Cree, cree, cree!

La, la, la!

When they finished,

the park was silent.

Not a bee buzzed.

Then the cheers began!

The beetle band won!

When Saul was better,

the beetles left.

Tucker tried hard not to cry.

"Don't worry, Tucker,"

said Harry.

"If you miss the noise at night,

I'll learn to snore!"

8/2013 $9.79